Dedicated to the little girls who will grow up to be powerful women, the boys who will become men, and the parents who try their best but still sometimes feel inadequate. May you give yourself grace and know you're doing a far better job than you give yourself credit for.

And to my own children, June, Thaddeus, and Knox,

thank you

for inspiring this book; may you always remember how much I love you.

Lessons
I Hope to Teach My Daughter

Published by Lacey Nagao
Nagao.lacey@gmail.com
Find her on instagram
@lacey-Nagao

Book design and Illustrations: Megan Welker Find more of her work on instagram @ahintofpixiedustpaints

Library of Congress Control Number: 2021923297

ISBN: 9780578916286 (paperback)
ISBN: 9780578916293 (ebook)

First printing 2021

LESSONS

I Hope to Teach My Daughter

Written by Lacey Nagao and Illustrated by Megan Welker

From the moment you were placed in my arms, I promised that I would do everything I could to keep you **safe,** help you **be happy,** and **ALWAYS love you.** Sometimes that means Mom will do things that you might not like, or you might not understand immediately. Just remember, this is what "Momma's do," and we do it because we LOVE you.

Sometimes life is hard, sometimes it's scary, and sometimes it can even seem strangely unfair. Momma has experienced all of these feelings before, and I know that as you grow up, you will too, L i t t l e   B u g .

One day, I hope you will look back and see that while I wasn't perfect, we sure learned a lot together on this roller coaster ride called "life." From the belly laughs, to the sleepless nights, you have taught me more than you will ever KNOW.

As I've been watching you grow up, I often sit back and smile. I am so proud of the person you are becoming! I'm raising someone who is going to do **BIG** things in this world. **You are a leader!** Being a leader comes with a lot of responsibility though and a lot of "trial and error." Here are a few, **"Life Lessons from Momma"** that I hope you'll try to always r e m e m b e r . . . .

I hope you will always be the type of person who cares more about how they treat the kid sitting alone at the lunch table, than **how many points you can score** on the basketball court.
...

(And remember, the kid sitting alone at the lunch table is just as special in God's eyes as the star basketball player! **Make sure to treat them that way).**

~~One day~~ you will mess up.

Actually, there might be lots of days you "mess up." You will make mistakes; please come tell me. Let's talk about it. I will help you figure out the best s o l u t i o n .

I hope you always remember there is nothing you CAN OR CAN'T do to make me love you anymore; I already love you as much as a Momma can love...

INFINITELY.

Sometimes even moms mess up; I hope you will FORGIVE me on those hard days. I'm still learning too.

I hope you will always be nice to the new kid at school, even if it's scary to meet someone new. **Remember to shake their hand, smile, and say,** "Hello! Would you like to play together?"

Words can hurt. Be careful what you say to people. There will be times that you might overhear a group gossiping about another person. I hope you will always be the person who stands up for others. **Nothing good ever comes from gossip or jealousy. Ever.**

If you find yourself "in the wrong," say sorry and **admit your mistake.** F O R G I V E yourself and forgive others.

I don't care if you're the best at something. (In fact, most the time, you WON'T be the best because God created everyone with different talents).

I DO care if you are the hardest worker in the room though. Always try YOUR very best. Always commit to working hard, even on the days that you don't want to. If you do this, you'll be successful. ALWAYS.

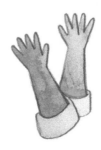

When someone does something great - like a teammate gets a new gymnastics skill or a student in class gets the best test score - **I hope you are the first person to tell them, "Great job!"** I hope you cheer for them, clap for them, and are truly

HAPPY FOR THEM.
Never forget that you **WANT** to surround yourself with people who do their best work and challenge you; that's how you'll become the

best version of YOU!
Most people are excited to share their talents and we can learn A LOT from each other.

I hope you fail sometimes; b e c a u s e if you **FAIL,** that means you tried something **NEW,** even if it means you fall on your face and get some scraped elbows and knees.

All the best people
are a little weird.
Keep being YOU.
Keep believing in
yourself, and NEVER
think any dream
is TOO CRAZY.

I know you love your mom more than anything and think I am amazing and super smart and know **EVERYTHING** right now. I'm quite possibly the smartest person in the whole wide world, right?!

...

Well, this is your warning that there will come a day, likely when you are getting to be about 14-years-old, that **you might not think that anymore.** You may even think that your mom has gone crazy. I want you to know that that's okay - just remember that I warned you; you'll come back and thank me for all my crazy rules one day.

P R O M I S E .

Your body is BEAUTIFUL for all it is able to do! **Be kind to it.** Be thankful for it.

Our bodies come in all shapes **and** sizes **and** colors.
That's what makes **YOU** unique and beautiful.

I hope you remember that it is always okay to **STAND UP** for yourself and your **FAMILY** . You have a mouth for a reason. Ask questions. Say what you are thinking. Stay curious. Don't let anyone tell you **DIFFERENTLY** .

You are **stronger** than you think you are, Little Bug.

The world needs

I promise I will always be here to remind you of that.

s t r o n g   g i r l s .

When something gets hard and
you want to quit,

I hope you will be the
person who keeps going.

Everything worthwhile takes
time and is HARD
s o m e t i m e s .

When you are sad, come tell me. I want to hear about your day. I want to help you. Remember that momma has bad days too; some fresh air and a bubble bath can fix most things though. Even when you feel all alone on the worst of days - you are never alone.

BE KIND

to all the animals and the Earth. It is your s w e e t , innocent spirit that will forever be **one of my favorite things about** Y O U .

People **will always remember** how you
t r e a t e d   t h e m ;
so **treat them** with RESPECT.
There is never a reason to be
u n k i n d   t o   s o m e o n e .

Remember, you are a
Child of God.
You are special. You are
loved. You are worthy.
You are enough.
ALWAYS.

Finally, I hope you know that while I will always do my best to teach you everything I possibly can,

YOU are actually the person who is teaching ME.

From your eyes, I have learned how to love unconditionally, how to laugh, how to find happiness, how to persevere, how to be a better person, how to dance barefoot, and how to DREAM. For that, I am forever grateful.

I'm excited to see where life takes you Little Bug ... Momma will be watching.
....

P.S. ... Don't forget to call me from time to time!

"Jump off
The Beam
Flip off the Bars
Follow your
Dreams and
reach for the
stars!"

-June Nagao

CPSIA information can be obtained
at www.ICGtesting.com
Printed in the USA
LVHW071802130122
708508LV00006B/119

9 780578 916286